Dear Parents and Educators,

Welcome to Penguin Young Readers! As parents and educators, you know that each child develops at his or her own pace—in terms of speech, critical thinking, and, of course, reading. Penguin Young Readers recognizes this fact. As a result, each Penguin Young Readers book is assigned a traditional easy-to-read level (1–4) as well as a Guided Reading Level (A–P). Both of these systems will help you choose the right book for your child. Please refer to the back of each book for specific leveling information. Penguin Young Readers features esteemed authors and illustrators, stories about favorite characters, fascinating nonfiction, and more!

| Star Wars®: The Clone Wars™ | LEVEL **2** |
| The Secret Villain | GUIDED READING LEVEL **I** |

This book is perfect for a **Progressing Reader** who:
• can figure out unknown words by using picture and context clues;
• can recognize beginning, middle, and ending sounds;
• can make and confirm predictions about what will happen in the text; and
• can distinguish between fiction and nonfiction.

Here are some **activities** you can do during and after reading this book:
• Character Traits: There are many characters in this story. They are listed on page 4. On a separate sheet of paper, list the names of each character and words that describe them. For example, you could write "Count Dooku" and "evil."
• Make Predictions: What do you think will happen to Savage? Will he find his brother? If so, what will they do to become the new Sith Lords?

Remember, sharing the love of reading with a child is the best gift you can give!

—Bonnie Bader, EdM
  Penguin Young Readers program

D1280312

*Penguin Young Readers are leveled by independent reviewers applying the standards developed by Irene Fountas and Gay Su Pinnell in *Matching Books to Readers: Using Leveled Books in Guided Reading*, Heinemann, 1999.

Penguin Young Readers
Published by the Penguin Group
Penguin Group (USA) Inc., 375 Hudson Street, New York, New York 10014, USA
Penguin Group (Canada), 90 Eglinton Avenue East, Suite 700, Toronto, Ontario M4P 2Y3, Canada
(a division of Pearson Penguin Canada Inc.)
Penguin Books Ltd., 80 Strand, London WC2R 0RL, England
Penguin Group Ireland, 25 St. Stephen's Green, Dublin 2, Ireland
(a division of Penguin Books Ltd.)
Penguin Group (Australia), 250 Camberwell Road, Camberwell, Victoria 3124, Australia
(a division of Pearson Australia Group Pty. Ltd.)
Penguin Books India Pvt. Ltd., 11 Community Centre, Panchsheel Park, New Delhi—110 017, India
Penguin Group (NZ), 67 Apollo Drive, Rosedale, Auckland 0632, New Zealand
(a division of Pearson New Zealand Ltd.)
Penguin Books (South Africa) (Pty.) Ltd., 24 Sturdee Avenue, Rosebank,
Johannesburg 2196, South Africa

Penguin Books Ltd., Registered Offices: 80 Strand, London WC2R 0RL, England

This book is published in partnership with LucasBooks, a division of Lucasfilm Ltd.

ISBN 978-0-448-45744-4   10 9 8 7 6 5 4 3 2

STAR WARS
THE CLONE WARS

THE SECRET VILLAIN

by Rob Valois

Penguin Young Readers
An Imprint of Penguin Group (USA) Inc.
LucasBooks

Here are some *Clone Wars* terms that might help you along the way.

 **Count Dooku** was a **Sith Lord** and enemy of the **Jedi**. He was a Master of the dark side of the **Force**.

 **Ventress** was **Count Dooku**'s student. She hoped to become a **Sith Lord** like her teacher.

 The **Nightsisters** were powerful witches. They lived on a faraway planet.

 **Savage** was a strong warrior. He was from the same planet as the **Nightsisters**.

 The **Jedi** were protectors of the galaxy. It was their job to stop **Count Dooku**.

 The **Force** was an energy that gave the **Jedi** and **Sith Lords** their special power.

The evil **Count Dooku** was a
Sith Lord, and his student was
named **Ventress**.

Ventress served her Master well and always tried her best to do what he asked.

But the **Jedi** were winning too

many battles.

He told **Ventress** that she could

no longer be his student.

Count Dooku went to see

the **Nightsisters.**

They were a group of witches

who lived on a faraway planet.

They had found a new student

for **Count Dooku**.

This new student's name

was **Savage**.

The **Nightsisters** used their magic to give him special powers that made him very strong.

He quickly became the
perfect student.

Savage was now ready to fight alongside his new Master.

Count Dooku sent him into battle

against the **Jedi**.

The **Jedi** were no match
for **Savage**'s power.
Count Dooku was happy
with his new student.

Count Dooku didn't know that the witches had tricked him. **Ventress** had been **Savage**'s secret Master all along.

She planned to defeat

Count Dooku and take

his place as a **Sith Lord**.

But **Count Dooku** was more

powerful than she had thought.

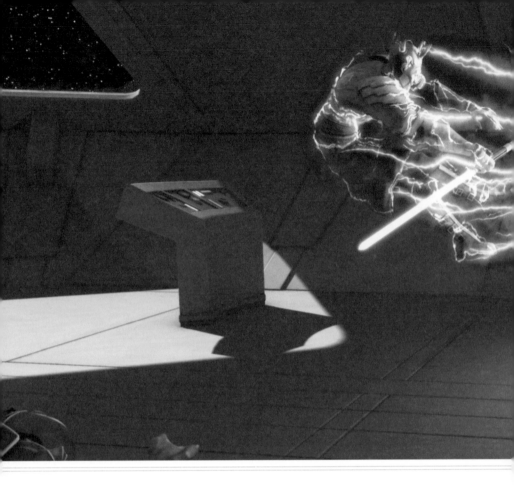

The **Sith Lord** was able to use the dark side of the **Force** to defeat **Savage**.

Ventress tried as hard as she could to battle her former Master.

But he was even too powerful for her to defeat.

Ventress lost the battle and had to go into hiding.

Count Dooku was not happy.

He sent his armies out to

find **Savage**.

Savage had escaped and headed

back to the **Nightsisters**.

The **Nightsisters** told **Savage**

that he was not alone.

Savage had a brother.

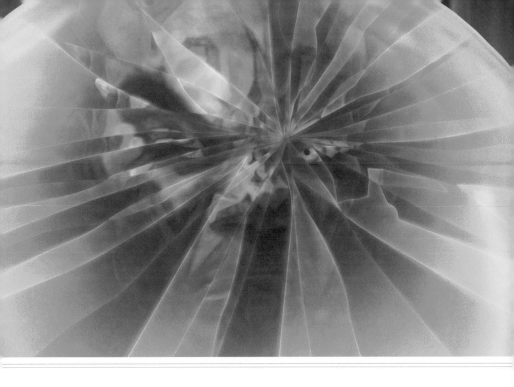

His brother had been a **Sith Lord**
until he was defeated by the **Jedi**.

Savage left to go find his brother.
Maybe one day they would return
and become the new **Sith Lords**
of the galaxy.